THE QUEST FOR THE SILVER FEATHER

A CHOOSE YOUR OWN ADVENTURE STORY

Written and Illustrated by Andrea Edwards

Creating magical journeys one choice at a time.

Willowsong
Press

Willowsong
Press

Dedication

To my family—Ben, Aubrey, and Ian—for your
unwavering support in every adventure.

To my sister, Sara, who inspired me to write my
own story.

And to my nephews—Blake, Julian, and Arlen—
thank you for listening to my early drafts with such
delight and suspense.

How to Read This Book

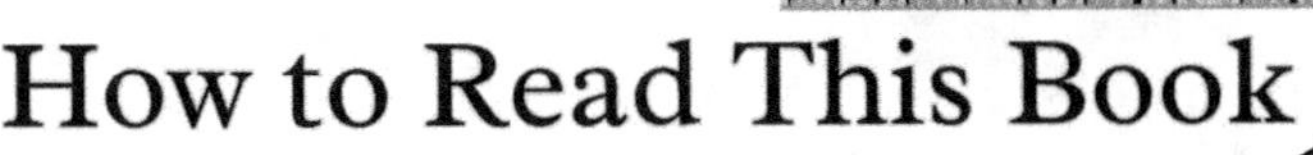

This isn't just a story—
it's a magical maze of choices, secrets, and surprises!

At the end of each section, **YOU** get to decide
what happens next.

Will you defeat a dragon?
Sneak past a grumpy librarian?
Enter a mysterious dark tunnel?

Every decision leads to a new twist, so read it again
and again to explore every wild path!

The journey starts now.

Open the book, grab your courage
(and maybe a sandwich),
and let the adventure begin!

Flip the page and find out—your adventure awaits!

THE QUEST FOR THE SILVER FEATHER

A CHOOSE YOUR OWN ADVENTURE STORY

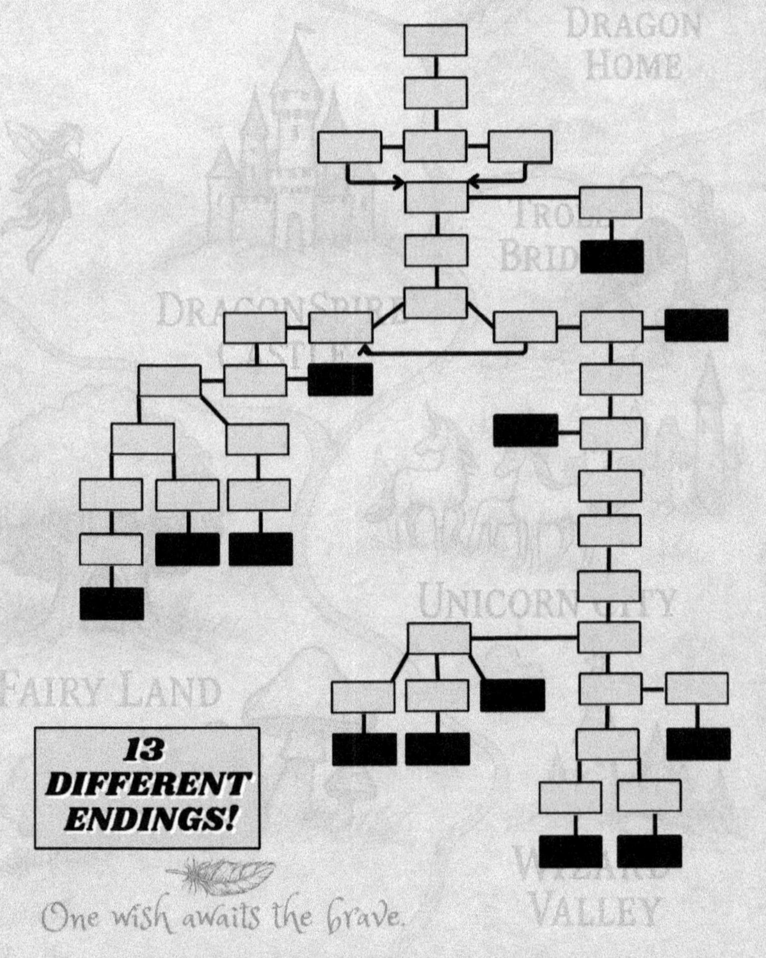

13 DIFFERENT ENDINGS!

One wish awaits the brave.

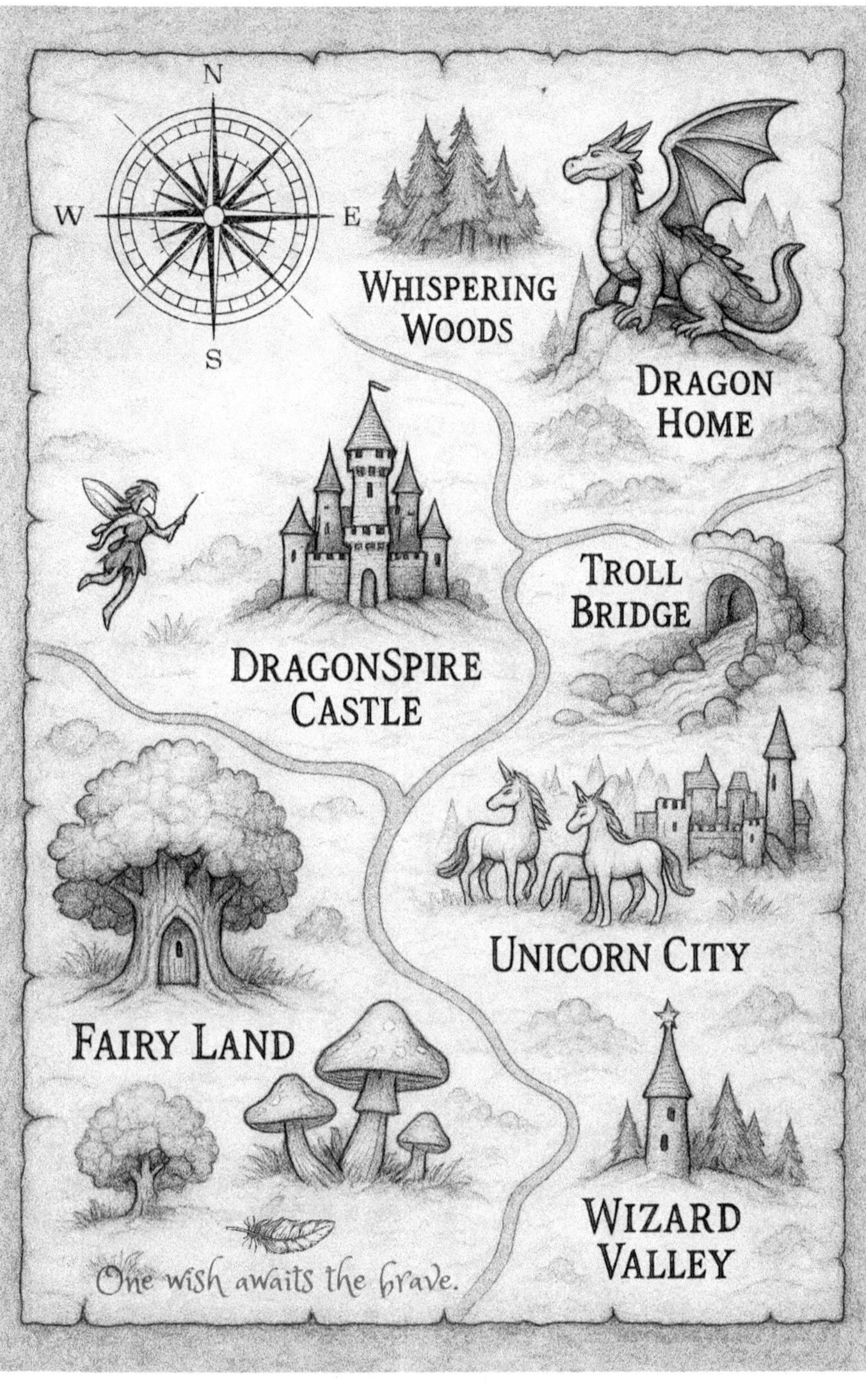

N
W
E
S
WHISPERING
WOODS
DRAGON
HOME
TROLL
BRIDGE
DRAGONSPIRE
CASTLE
UNICORN CITY
FAIRY LAND
WIZARD
VALLEY
One wish awaits the brave.

☁ The Rainy Day ☁

"Today's perfect for a hike!" you say—right before it starts to drizzle.

You've already hiked every trail in the woods behind your house. Twice. Maybe three times. You never go anywhere without your trusty red backpack, your half-broken compass, and a crust-free peanut butter and jelly sandwich.

But today? It's raining.

So you change plans and head to the town library.

You dash through the light rain like a soggy movie hero and swing open the heavy wooden doors of the old brick library.

Inside, it's warm and dry. It smells like books and old paper—*Nice*, you think.

You shake the water from your sleeves like a wet puppy and head straight to your favorite section—Fantasy.

Wizards, dragons, magical forests? Yes, please.

You grin, ready for a new adventure—just not the kind you expected.

As you look at the dusty shelves, something catches your eye.

A big green book with the title **DragonSpire** on the spine. You look closer at the book. Is that... glitter? No, wait... scales?

You reach for the book—**click**!

Suddenly, part of the shelf swings open like it's been waiting just for you. *Did pulling on the book just open a hidden room?* you wonder.

"Yep," you say as you answer your own question.

Behind it is a tiny secret room lit by a flickering lightbulb. Your heart flips with joy. **"Secret rooms are the best,"** you whisper to yourself.

Inside, lying in the corner like it's been napping for a hundred years, is a leather book with a glowing silver feather on the cover.

You wipe off the dust on the cover and read the title: **Whispering Woods: Tales of Myths and Magic**

"Achoo!" you sneeze, as you wave your hand to clear the air. When the dust settles, you open the book carefully.

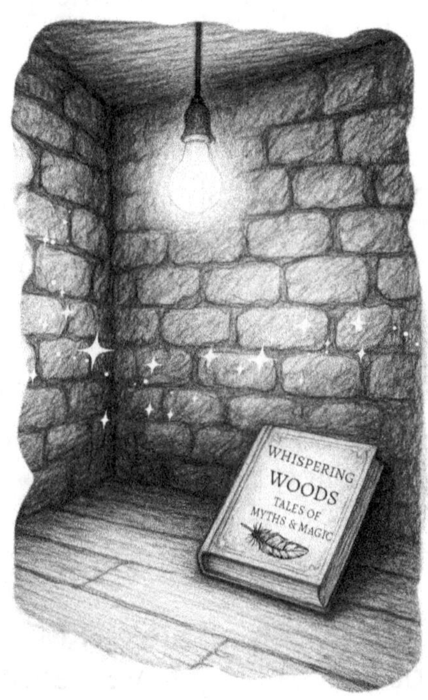

A torn map floats out of the first page and lands in your hands like a paper plane. At the bottom of the map, you spot a drawn silver feather and under it the words:

One wish awaits the brave.

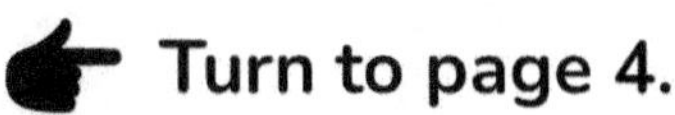 **Turn to page 4.**

You slide the book and map into your backpack as quietly as you can. *No one will miss them*, you think. And just like that, the real adventure begins.

You leave the secret room and curl up in your favorite spot—the one with the squishy old cushion and the colorful glass windows that make everything look like it's been dipped in rainbow syrup.

You unzip your backpack, glance around like a spy, and—Freeze.

Movement in the mystery section.

It's Ms. Nelson, the librarian. She's silent, sneaky and possibly part cat.

Your heart thumps. Suddenly—**CLANG!**

A loud crash comes from the other side of the library. Ms. Nelson gasps and zooms away like she just caught someone throwing books.

Phew. You breath deeply.

You pull **Whispering Woods: Tales of Myths and Magic** from your backpack. The silver feather on the cover shines like a faded star.

"Whoa," you whisper, flipping it open.

A strange feeling comes over you. *Why does the book feel like it's calling to you?*

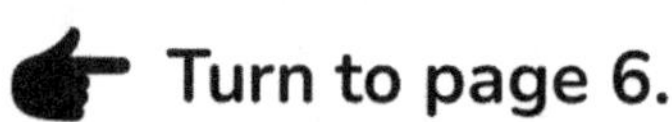 **Turn to page 6.**

Top Secret Stairs

You turn the pages of the book until a drawing catches your eye. You see words written and a big X—just like a treasure map.

The second floor? That place is usually off-limits. Your eyes light up. **"An adventure right here? I'm in!"** you say excitedly.

You tuck the book into your backpack and reach for your peanut butter and jelly sandwich...

You stop yourself. *Nope. Saving that for an emergency.*

You sneak to the bottom of the creaky old staircase. A thick rope blocks the way up like it's guarding treasure. You glance around and the coast is clear.

You duck under the rope and tiptoe upstairs. *I hope Ms. Nelson doesn't catch me,* you worry.

At the top, you find one big, dusty room. It has an old desk, some shelves, and a painting of a giant castle with a dragon. Under the painting is a name plate that reads **DragonSpire Castle.**

You grin. **"I wonder what's hiding in this room?"**

Definitely not just dust bunnies.

Do you:

 **Check out the desk? (Turn to page 10)**

Check out the painting? (Turn to page 14)

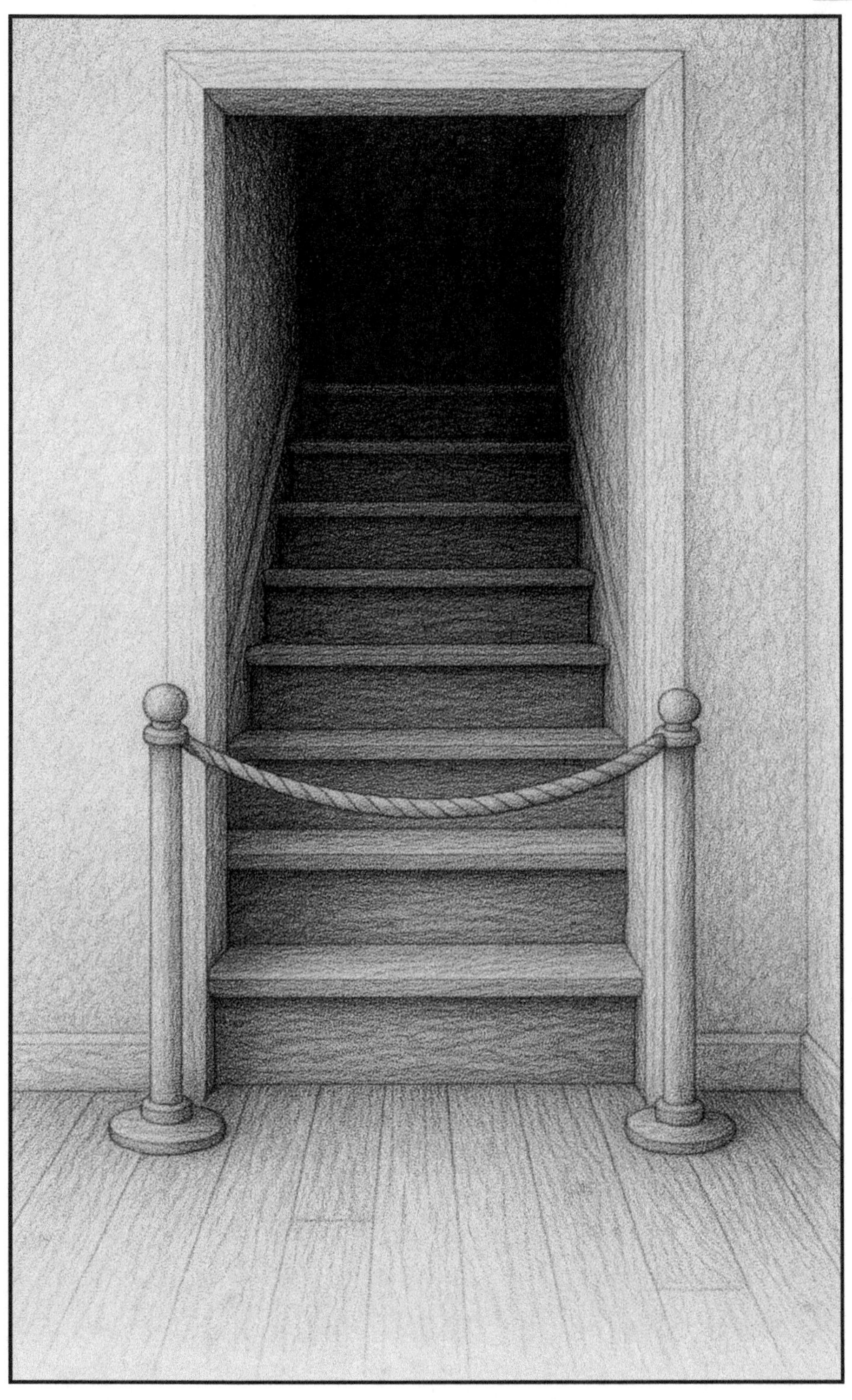

The Sky Ride Surprise

You reach out and touch the glowing orb—because, of course, that seems like a good idea, right?

Suddenly—**ZAP!** A burst of bright light hits you like a lightning bolt.

In the blink of an eye, you disappear from the room and land in a huge nest high up in a tree. *How did I get here?* you wonder. You are tangled in twigs, crunchy leaves, and what looks like Grandma's missing slippers, all poking you in weird places.

One minute you're looking at the nest. The next minute, you're soaring above the treetops. The sky is filled with color, like someone spilled a box of crayons. Down below, you see a world of magical creatures: a swarm of sparkling fairies doing loops, and a pair of unicorns playing tag near a rainbow stream.

As you fly through the sky, you feel something wrapped around your waist.

You
    look
        down...

TALONS?!

Big, sharp talons that you definitely shouldn't try to high-five.

You look up and gasp.

An enormous silver eagle is staring down at you. With strong wings, it carries you gently through the sky.

You hope you're not a snack, you think nervously.

Soon, something large appears in the distance. It's growing clearer, taller, fancier...

It's a castle!

Not just any castle. It's the very same one you saw in the glowing orb and painting in the library!

This can't be luck, you think, your stomach doing a backflip. *That must be* **DragonSpire Castle!**

After a thrilling flight filled with swoops, spins, and one crazy sneeze from the eagle (don't ask), it lands and sets you down gently on the ground—not far from the huge castle.

You wobble a little. Your hair's a mess. But you can't stop grinning.

Okay, you think, *this just got awesome.*

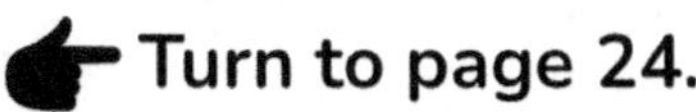
Turn to page 24.

 The Desk

You scan the room and tap your finger against your chin as you think for a moment.

"There is something strange about this desk," you say to yourself in your best detective voice.

It looks like an old writing desk with worn wood, little cubbies for letters, and ink stains on the top.

Honestly, it smells like a mix of pencil shavings and old lunches—Gross.

You open one of the drawers and say, **"Nothing..."**

You try the next one. **"Still empty."**

Just as you turn away, you notice scratch marks on the wooden floor like someone has pushed the desk back and forth a lot.

"What's hiding behind you?" you ask the desk.

You lean your shoulder into the desk and give it a shove. It doesn't move.

Not even a wiggle.

With a sigh, you plop down on the matching wooden chair.

"Think, think…" you mumble, tapping your head. **"Didn't Grandma's desk have a secret spot where she kept candy?"**

You lean forward and look at each drawer. One looks more worn than the rest.

"Aha!" you say, sounding a little too proud. You pull out the drawer and slip your hand inside.

Click!

Your fingers hit a small hidden button! Suddenly, the whole desk jerks back fast toward you with a loud scratching noise! You leap out of the way like a ninja, your heart pounding.

"Whoa! That was close! I almost became a pancake!" you say, laughing.

Behind the desk, where a solid wall once stood, there's now a dark tunnel.

"Well," you say, grinning like someone about to open a big birthday present, **"Let's see where this leads."**

You stand up, take a deep breath, and step forward into the tunnel's dark mouth.

"If there's a giant spider in there, I'm turning right back around," you say with a nervous grin.

 **Venture down the tunnel. (Turn to page 20)**

(Turn to page 20)

✦ The Fairy ✧

You step off the drawbridge into the castle's wide, quiet courtyard. You can almost imagine what it would have looked like long ago. Stalls stacked high with fruit, toys, and sparkly treasures—bustling with people and mystical creatures.

Now, though, everything is empty and still.

A soft rustle comes from behind a broken cart. You freeze, listening. Could someone—or something—be hiding here?

Just then, you hear a flutter of wings behind you. You spin around, thinking that Jax followed you into the castle, but you come face-to-face with what must be a fairy.

She is three times the size of Jax, dressed in tattered green clothes, her hair wild and eyes as green as grass. She raises a tiny wand and points it straight at your nose.

"You are not allowed here!" she squeaks in an angry little voice. **"Stop—or I'll turn you into a toad!"**

Your heart pounds, but you take a deep breath and find your courage.

"I'm just a traveler," you say softly. **"I'm new to this place. Do you know where I can find the dragon?"**

The fairy flutters her wings and laughs. **"Are you sure you want to find the dragon?"**

She glances at you with a sparkle in her eyes and giggles, **"You might be next on his menu if you don't leave fast!"**

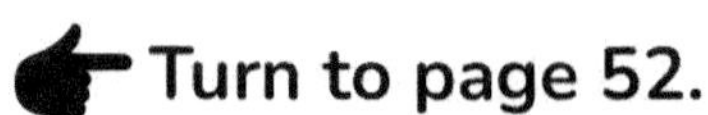

You nod quickly—and your legs start moving away on their own.

"I understand," you say, walking back toward the gate.

You decide you need to find another way into the castle.

👉 **Turn to page 52.**

 The Painting

You decide to walk over to the painting. It shows a big castle with a dark moat around it. Your eyes follow the stone walls up to the towers, where a dragon with shiny green scales flies above. It almost looks like it's grinning at you.

You spot something sparkling on the dragon's painted collar—it's a shiny red gem.

Why is there a real jewel on the painting? you wonder.

Gathering your courage, you carefully reach out and touch the gem.

Pop!

Creeeeak...

With a puff of dust, the nearby desk swings open—revealing a dark tunnel.

"**A secret passage!**" you exclaim, heart pounding. "**I wonder what might be hiding down there? Hopefully nothing with teeth...**"

You take a deep breath, fix your backpack and crawl into the tunnel's dark mouth. You are ready for whatever strange, wild mystery waits ahead.

 **Venture down the tunnel. (Turn to page 20)**

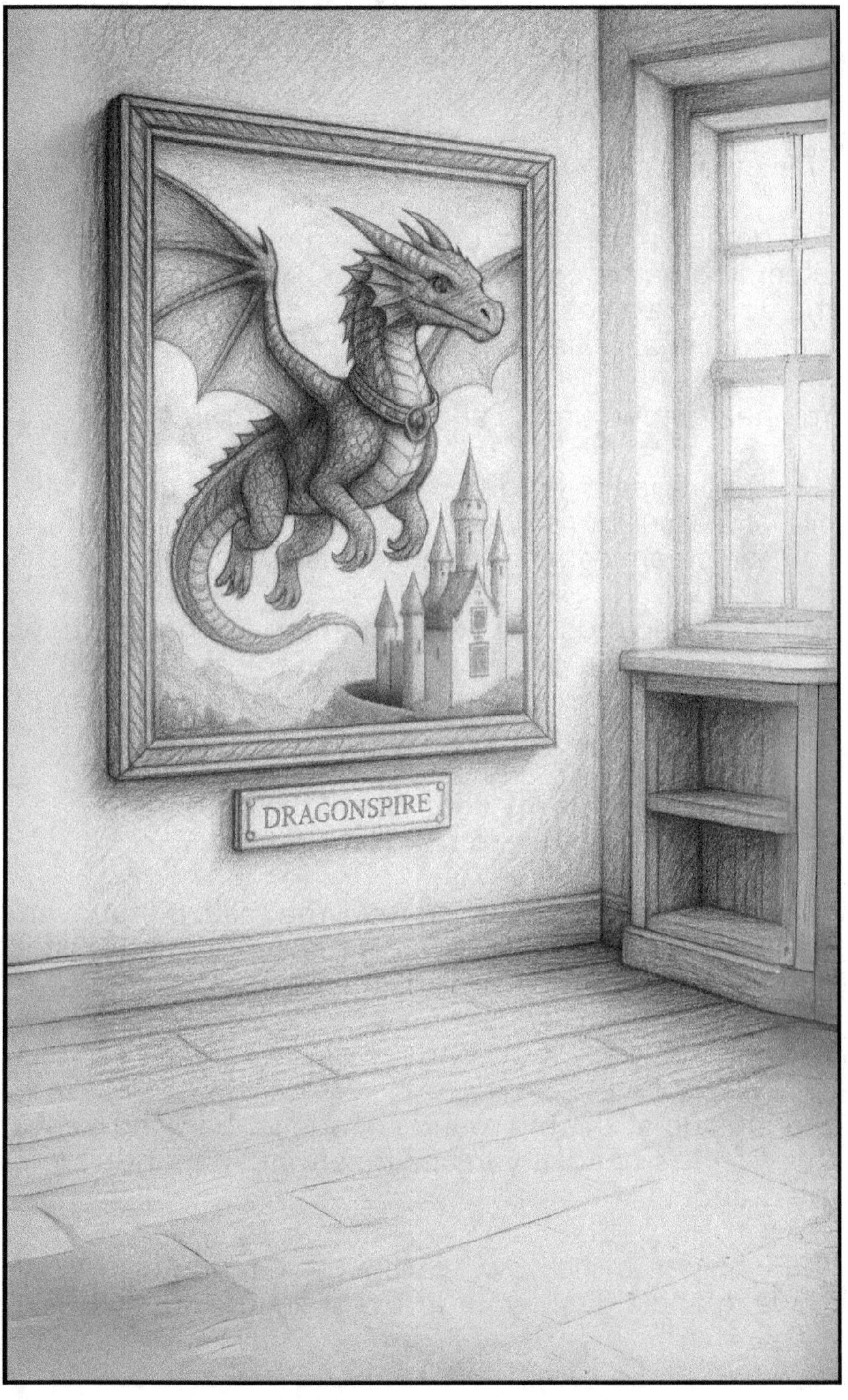
DRAGONSPIRE

⚜ The Dragon's Lair ⚜

The little fairy floats beside you, pointing down a twisty staircase.

"This way," she whispers, **"and be very quiet!"**

You go down the stairs until you come into a big room. Gleaming gems, coins, and other shiny things cover the floor like a sea of treasure. In the center, a silver and gold chandelier hangs on thick iron chains.

You hear a low rumble and turn toward the noise.

A huge dragon, with green scales, starts to stir on his pile of treasure. His wings shining in torchlight and you see steam coming from his nose.

Your heart pounds, but you remember the golden bow in your hand. You place an arrow on the string and pull it back. Just as you aim, the dragon's golden eyes snap open.

"Who dares enter my chamber?" the dragon growls, showing rows of shining sharp teeth.

Your hands start to shake in fear. You realize that even if you strike the dragon with your arrow, it might just bounce off his green scales.

You only have a few seconds to decide.

You look up at the big round chandelier hanging above the dragon's head. If you aim just right, it might trap the dragon.

You whisper to the bow, **"Strike the chandelier!"** With a twang and a flash, your arrow soars up—**CLANG!**

It smashes the giant steel chandelier free. The big light crashes down, its chains twisting, and lands on the dragon.

The dragon roars, shaking the cave walls and roars, **"Why have you trapped me?"**

You step forward, holding your bow steady and looking the dragon in his eyes.

"You are hurting the creatures of this land with your fiery breath," you say firmly.

The dragon looks at you in surprise and then grumbles, **"I'm not harming the creatures."**

The fairy whispers in your ear, **"Don't believe him. He's tricky and a liar."**

The dragon's great head lifts higher.

A grin starts to creep across the corner of his large toothy mouth.

Just then, the dragon shakes and breaks free of the chandelier.

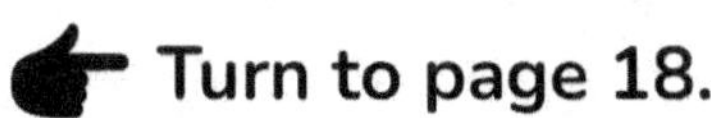 **Turn to page 18.**

⚬ **The Dragon Bubbles** ⚬

The dragon **ROARS** and puffs his chest for a mighty blast of fire! You feel the heat on your face.

Quickly, you pull the silver feather from your pocket and whisper, **"Turn the dragon's fire into bubbles."**

With a whoosh, shiny bubbles float out of the dragon's mouth instead of fire! The dragon blinks in surprise, blows a few more bubbles and flaps his great wings. He soars out of the castle—zipping through a secret exit hidden behind a dusty old curtain (who knew dragons used secret doors!).

The moment the dragon is gone—**CRACK**! Sparkles shoot from the fairies wand. You both leap a foot in the air, well maybe two feet.

"Yikes!" the fairy squeaks, her wings buzzing like a scared bumblebee.

Just then, the fairy realizes what has happened and shouts, **"The dragon has left and the wizard's spell has been broken! I am free!"**

You and the fairy jump up and down, cheering. Then your smile fades—you've used your one wish, and now you can't wish yourself home.

The fairy sees your joy turn to sadness, and then to fear.

She flutters close and places a tiny hand on your shoulder. **"Thank you for freeing me,"** she says softly. **"I am so very thankful for your kindness, I would like to repay you by sending you home."**

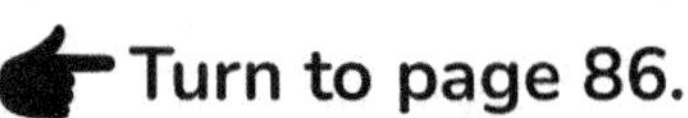

"Please!" you say gratefully.

The fairy asks, **"Are you ready?"**

You nod yes.

The fairy raises her magic wooden wand and speaks one word: **"Home!"**

In a flash of color and a soft pop...

☛ **Turn to page 86.**

🍄 The Tunnel 🍄

You crawl into the tight dark tunnel behind the desk.

"Yuck," you mumble as your hand slides over a slimy stone. It's too tight to stand, so you wiggle forward like a worm with a backpack.

The glow from the library fades, but ahead you see mushrooms! Tiny blue ones that glow like nightlights for bugs. They cover the tunnel walls and you follow them as the path twists and turns.

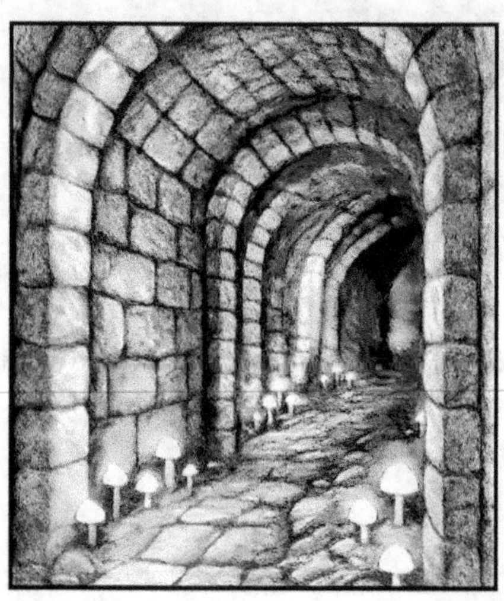

Then you see it. A soft light and a small room up ahead. In the middle sits a glass orb on a table, calling to you with a gentle hum.

You stretch your legs as you exit the tunnel. **"Finally! I can stand again,"** you sigh.

But then—Whoosh! The tunnel behind you seals shut with a stone slam.

No going back now.

You step closer to the orb and peek inside. A swirling image appears: a mighty dragon flying around a familiar castle.

Suddenly, a deep voice echoes out of the orb: **"Come and defeat the dragon. It is your only way home."**

You leap back in fright. **"My only way home!"** you gasp.

Before you can even think about it, the floor rumbles and... **Click!**

A stone door slides open behind the orb, showing a twisty set of stairs covered in green vines. Your heart beats fast as you stare at the steps.

You shake your head in disbelief. *There seems to be a lot of secret doors around here!* You think to yourself with curiosity.

You imagine a sign that says:

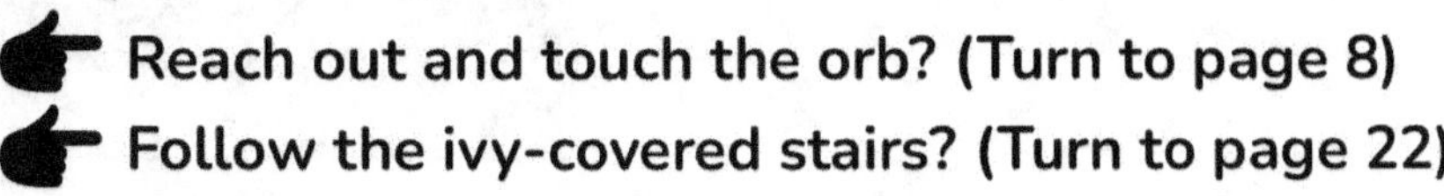

Do you:

Reach out and touch the orb? (Turn to page 8)

Follow the ivy-covered stairs? (Turn to page 22)

 The Stairs 

You follow the twisting staircase until you step into a dark forest. *It's quiet—too quiet.* You get the creepy feeling you're not alone.

Something is totally watching you, you think, looking around. You hope it's not a troll with an anger problem.

Your heart thumps like a drum as a shape moves in the tall grass beside you. Before you can run, a forest faun springs out!

He's half boy, half goat, and completely covered in dirt. From his waist down, he has furry legs that end in little hooves. From his waist up, you notice his hair's tangled —as if he got stuck in a bush full of twigs. He looks like a human boy with bright eyes that sparkle with mischief.

"Ah, a brave traveler!" he giggles, his voice high and playful. **"Tell me, what are you doing in these woods?"**

Startled, you respond, **"I am here to find the dragon. Can you help me?"**

The faun's eyes narrow. His smile fades like melting ice cream.

"You won't be meeting the dragon ever," he says with a sneer. **The wizard has told me to stop anyone from getting near DragonSpire Castle."**

Um... a wizard? And definitely not the friendly guide you were hoping for, you think nervously.

Your stomach twists into a pretzel. **"Stop me?"** you stammer.

With a sly grin, the faun lifts a tiny black flute to his lips and blows a sharp, squeaky note. Just then— **RUMBLE**!

The ground shakes beneath your feet. Loose stones hop like popcorn as the trail begins to twist and wiggle.

You back away slowly, arms flailing out to balance.

"Hey, that's not nice!" you shout.

Suddenly, the ground rumbles louder, and the path starts to shift. *You probably should've stayed in the library,* you think.

👉 **Turn to page 34.**

✦ The Wish ✦

Before the eagle flies away, it bows to you (yes, actually bows—like you're royalty) and says, **"One wish awaits the brave,"** in a deep voice.

One wish awaits the brave—there's that saying again. You think, but you can't place where you've seen or heard it before.

With its curved beak, the eagle gently plucks a small silver feather from under its wing and hands it to you.

You open your mouth to ask a ton of questions—*Do you get snacks? Can you fly now? What kind of wish is this?* —but the eagle takes off before you can say a single word.

The silver feather feels soft in your hand. You turn it over and it shimmers and sparkles in the light like it's been dipped in stardust.

You tuck it safely deep into your back pocket because you know it's important. Maybe, just maybe, it's the key to finding the dragon... and getting home.

Looking around, you realize something kind of terrible and you think, *You're lost. Like, really lost.*

Nothing looks familiar in these woods. Tall trees loom overhead and a narrow dirt path heads toward the direction of the castle. *It's probably full of danger, mystery, or biting troll, you fear.*

What should you do now? you wonder, as your stomach flops around like a fish out of water.

Just then, you spot a very strange looking tree. It's taller than any tree you've ever seen.

After looking up, your eyes move down the trunk and, to your surprise, there's a small door carved right into the tree!

Do you:

👉 **Head toward the castle? (Turn to page 28)**
👈 **Investigate the giant tree with the small door? (Turn to page 32)**

🎵 The Tune 🎵

Curiosity wins!

You push through the tiny door, and follow the humming tune down the secret passage.

With every step, the happy melody grows louder and it tickles your ears. One part even makes you giggle-snort for no reason at all.

A gentle voice sings:

"Tra-la-la, through leaf and night,
Brave heart shining golden bright.
Seek the path where shadows play—
Light the hope and find the way!"

At the end of the tunnel, you spot a small room lit with a warm, glowing light. The room smells like apples and wood. There, a little man sits on a wooden stool, singing the very same tune, while carving a dragon out of a block of wood.

He's no taller than a kid in kindergarten, with a long white beard that looks as soft as rabbit fur. He wears wire-rimmed glasses, and his tiny fingers move quickly and carefully as he works. His sparkling blue eyes flash up at you, and you notice something sticking out from under his leafy cap—pointy ears!

No way. An elf? A real one? you hope.

He sets down his carving knife and beams like a birthday cake full of candles.

"**Welcome! I am a Woodland Elf, and my name is Marrick,**" he says to you in a voice so cheerful it could make a grumpy cat smile.

"**The old stories said you would come to save our land one day,**" he says with a playful grin.

You blink. *Wait... saving the land? You? You still forget to take your morning vitamins.*

Marrick hops off his stool with a little bounce.

"**Legend says that whoever can solve my riddle will earn the power to bring peace back to all the creatures in this land,**" he says with a proud little smile.

Then he leans in, eyes twinkling like he knows something you don't—which, let's be honest—he probably does, and whispers, "**So... are you ready for my riddle?**"

Do you:

 **Try to solve the elf's riddle? (Turn to page 98)**

Head back to the castle instead?

(Turn to page 50)

You decide to skip the little door for now. The castle in the distance looks much more exciting.

The trail is narrow and twisty, and the plants are so tall that some of them hit you in the face. You push through like a mini jungle explorer.

After a while with no castle in sight, something zips past your ear—**BUZZ!**

"Yikes!" you yelp, swatting the air. Instead of flying away, something small bounces off your hand.

"Hey!" a tiny voice squeaks.

You freeze. *What was that?*

Floating right in front of you is a teeny-tiny guy with gold wings. He's no bigger than your finger, and he looks pretty annoyed.

"Watch where you're going!" he huffs. **"We sprites might be small, but we've got sharp teeth and I'm not afraid to use them!"**

"I'm sorry!" you say quickly. **"I thought you were a bug!"**

"Hmph. Not. A. Bug." The little guy crosses his arms. **"I'm Jax. A sprite. And today I'm collecting nectar from flowers."**

You smile at him, hoping to calm him down, and say, **"Nice to meet you, Jax. I'm looking for DragonSpire Castle."**

When Jax hears that, his eyes go wide. **"DragonSpire, well the unicorns' path you're on will lead you there!"**

"Wait... unicorns?" you say, looking down at the trail.

"Yep. But don't worry, they're not out this time of day—usually," Jax says, zooming around in the air.

"Look for a patch of red ferns, then turn left. You'll find the castle clearing after that," Jax tells you.

"Thanks, Jax! Good luck with the nectar!"

"Safe travels! Watch where you swat next time!" he calls, zipping away.

You keep walking around a few bends in the trail and —**Bam**! There it is. **DragonSpire Castle.** You stop and stare. **"Whoa..."** you whisper in disbelief.

You see tall stone towers, black flags with green dragons, a sparkling moat, and a wooden drawbridge. You take a deep breath and walk across the bridge, your heart thumping.

"Okay," you whisper, **"time to find the dragon."**

 **Turn to page 12.**

⚡ The Wingswift Shoes ⚡

You carefully lift the Wingswift Shoes out of their glass case. They look a bit worn, but you can almost feel their power humming under your fingers.

"Go on—try them!" the fairy says, flapping her wings beside you.

You slip off your own red sneakers and slide your feet into the plain brown leather ones. Immediately, a warm tingle runs up your legs.

You stand wobbly at first—but—suddenly, you're moving so fast the wall torches blur!

"Whoa!" you laugh, zooming around the library in a tight circle. **"I feel like a lightning bolt!"**

The fairy giggles. **"Careful, speedy—you don't want to crash into the walls!"**

You slow down and come to a gentle stop right in front of her. **"These are amazing! I can run anywhere as quick as the wind!"**

"Exactly," she says, tapping the case where the shoes once rested. **"With these on your feet, you can defeat the dragon in a flash."**

You grin, lacing up the shoe straps a little tighter. You would hate for the shoes to go flying off!

"All right—let's put these to the test," you say bravely.

You step forward and sprint toward the heavy oak door leading deeper into the castle, your heart pounding with excitement.

The fairy flies beside you, her laughter trailing behind like a happy song, as you rush off on your next big adventure.

Turn to page 94.

 The Tiny Door

You open your backpack and take out the map. You spread it out on a mossy rock and point to the tiny pictures. You say to yourself, **"Look—the Whispering Woods, the castle... and right here—"** you murmur, tapping next to the sketch of the tree with the tiny door.

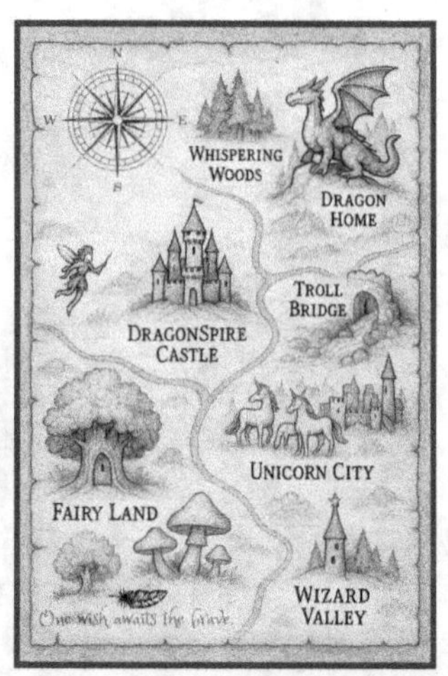

Yep. Tree with a door. Not even the weirdest thing today, you say to yourself.

"Better keep this safe," you whisper.

You carefully fold the map back up—well, kind of. It turns into a crumpled ball—but you do your best.

Then you look back at the tree. Your heart races. *Okay, this is either really magical—or about to get weird.*

"Here goes nothing," you say, raising your hand to knock on the tiny door.

Knock... Creak...

The door swings open all by itself!

Whoa. Automatic door. Fancy.

From somewhere inside, you hear a soft, joyful humming.

"What is that?" you wonder aloud.

You hear a melody floating through the air as if it's coming from a music box.

At the same time, the old castle in the distance seems to call out to you.

Do you:

 Follow the mystery tune? (Turn to page 26)

Go back towards the castle? (Turn to page 28)

The Earthquake

You freeze as the faun's grin grows wider—way too wide, like he knows a joke you won't find funny.

He lifts his flute to his lips to play another wild tune.

FWEEEEEEE!

Suddenly, the ground shakes harder, splitting open like a giant cracked cookie!

"HELP!" you yell, but it's too late.

A gust of wind and rolling stones knocks you off your feet and you tumble down into a dark hole.

Well, this isn't how you planned your day, you tell yourself.

For a moment, time stretches out like chewed gum. You hear only the faun's distant flute song around you.

Then... nothing. *No faun. No ground.* Your eyes snap open.

You're lying in your own bed, the early morning sun slipping through your curtains. You sit up, blinking, half expecting to see the faun playing the flute or glowing mushrooms.

But it's just your bedroom. **"Was that... real?"** you whisper.

You rub your sleepy eyes and stretch like a cat waking up from a nap.

You look up as something silver and shiny floats down. It twirls in the air, then drifts gently into your open hand.

It's a silver feather—just like the one on the book cover.

You smile. *Okay... that definitely wasn't a regular dream.* You sit back against your pillow, holding the feather.

You wonder what other mysteries are waiting for you next. You hope there'll be fewer holes and more snacks. Now to figure out what to do with this feather.

🏁 THE END 🏁

⚔ The Castle Armory ⚔

You and the little fairy slip through a big wooden door marked **Armory.** Torches flicker on stone walls, casting dancing shadows as you step inside. The room is cool and smells like old metal and leather. Shelves and racks are piled high with every kind of weapon you can imagine!

"Wow," you whisper. **"Look at all these swords!"**

The fairy flutters to a rack of gleaming blades. **"This one's a lion-tooth sword—sharp enough to slice through a witch's spell!"** she giggles, patting the sword's handle like a child pats a puppy.

You move on to a row of tall spears, their tips glinting like stars. **"Spears can reach past a dragon's huge claws,"** the fairy says, **"but they're heavy to carry."**

Next, you peek at a rack of knives and daggers. You think, *They're short and quick—but tricky to throw far.* You try twirling one in your hand, but it feels unsteady.

You sigh. **"Nothing here feels quite right..."**

The fairy's eyes light up. **"Wait! Over there!"**

She zooms across the room to a shining golden bow hung above a quiver of arrows tipped with crystal points. **"Legends say this bow never misses—the arrow always flies straight to the target you name!"**

Your heart skips a beat. You lift the bow. It's surprisingly light, and fits perfect in your hands. You pull back an arrow and it glows with a warm, gentle light.

"**This is perfect,**" you say. "**I'll need every bit of magic to face the dragon.**"

The fairy claps and sprinkles some blue fairy dust over the bow and arrows. "**May it guide your aim and your courage, brave friend!**"

With your new golden bow and enchanted arrows at your side, you and the fairy head to the castle's main hall—ready for what comes next.

 **Turn to page 16.**

 The Invisible Explorer

You lift the Invisibility Cloak from its case and drape it over your shoulders. A soft hush falls over the library as the fabric settles and starts to disappear. Then you look down at your hands... and they vanish!

You walk over to a tall, cracked mirror and look at yourself. The flickering torchlight is just bright enough for you to see the library's reflection but not yours.

"Wow," you whisper, voice echoing softly. **"I can't even see myself!"**

The fairy giggles and tugs at your sleeve. **"Perfect for sneaking,"** she says.

You creep through the library, your footsteps quieted by the soft carpet. The fairy flutters beside you.

"Where is the dragon?" you whisper.

She points up toward a set of twisty stairs. **"Follow me to the walkway at the top of the castle. The dragon loves to sit in the sun there at noon!"**

You tiptoe up the stairs, your heart thumping with excitement (and a little nervous). At last, you exit onto a broad stone ledge overlooking the courtyard.

Sunlight bathes everything in golden warmth and there, sprawled across the walkway, lies the dragon. His emerald scales glisten like jewels as it soaks up the rays.

 **Turn to page 40.**

🐀 The Rat 🐀

Your heart pounds. The cloak billows softly behind you as you edge forward.

"Ready?" the fairy whispers.

You nod, hardly daring to breathe.

Just then, the dragon's deep voice rumbles—
"Who goes there?"

Its huge head lifts, and it sniffs the air with a great snort. **"I can smell you, little rats!"**

The fairy ducks behind a round tower pillar. You freeze, hidden by your cloak, as the dragon's tail whips around with a loud **SWISH!**

You duck and roll just in time as his tail whizzes over your head. It stands tall, claws clicking on the stone floor, towering above you. You feel his hot breath on your face.

Taking a deep breath, you sprint under the dragon's belly, pulling the silver feather from your pocket. As you dart past his hind leg, you whisper to the feather —**"Turn the dragon into a rat!"**

In a flash of silver light, the dragon lets out a surprised **SQUEAK!**—and suddenly shrinks into a tiny, scaly green rat that darts past you and scurries down the stairs.

You skitter to a stop. The fairy appears beside you, clapping her hands. **"You did it!"** she cries.

You pull the hood back, revealing your wide, happy grin. **"We did it together,"** you tell her, tucking the cloak around your shoulders.

The rat (formerly dragon) disappears through a crack in the wall, leaving only the soft echo of his squeak behind.

You and the fairy laugh together, ready for your next magical adventure...

Or maybe...
you're ready to head
home safely.

🏁 **THE END** 🏁

❓ The Doors ❓

You look down at the little fairy and feel a tug in your heart. You want to help her find her way home, but you also remember that defeating the dragon might be the key to getting you home.

You take a deep breath and say, **"I think if we can beat the dragon, your spell might break. Then we can both get what we want."**

The fairy's wings flutter so fast that it looks like she's surrounded by a swirling blue fan. **"Yes! Yes!"** she cries. **"I'll help you any way I can!"**

She swoops in close and whispers, **"Did anyone ever tell you that the one who holds a silver feather is granted one wish?"**

You look at the fairy in surprise. **"No, thank you for telling me! Now I know what the eagle meant by 'One wish awaits the brave'."**

The fairy smiles, looking proud of herself, and says, **"But first, we need something powerful to face the dragon."**

You nod. **"Where should we look?"**

The fairy leads you into the castle and points toward two great doors down a large hallway. One is marked **Armory** and the other is marked **Library.**

She tugs at your sleeve and grins. **"The armory holds mighty swords, spears, and shields—but the library... who knows what magical surprises hide among its scrolls?"**

Do you:

Head to the armory? (Turn to page 36)
Head to the library? (Turn to page 48)

🏰 The Castle 🏰

You set off down the curvy dirt path, leaves crunching under your shoes and your backpack bouncing with every step.

The forest is so dark and twisty, it looks like someone designed it for scary stories. After what seems like a thousand hours, but is really just one—you finally see light ahead!

The path opens into a flower-dotted meadow so bright and sparkly you almost expect a family of fairies to pop out.

There it stands: The castle. *Not just any castle—* **DragonSpire Castle!**

"**Wow**," you murmur, your voice barely louder than a breeze. **"It's even more enormous than I ever dreamed."**

You step onto the wooden drawbridge, hearing the ropes creak softly underfoot. The castle's great arched gate is just ajar, as if someone left it open to say, *Come in… if you dare!*

Your heart races and your cheeks warm with excitement. **"All right,"** you whisper, **"this is it. Time to face the dragon."**

You take one step across the drawbridge…

      then another step…

          and then…

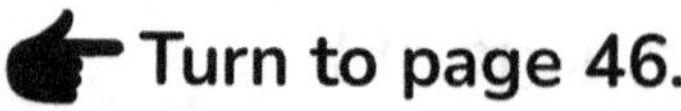 **Turn to page 46.**

DRAGONSPIRE

🛒 The Chamber 🛒

You step into the castle courtyard, and think, *whoa—this place looks really old.*

Old broken market stalls and empty wooden boxes line the floor. You pause, imagining what it must have been like long ago: villagers chatting, merchants shouting **"Two for one dragonberries!"** and maybe someone trying to sell slightly used wizard hats.

Ahead, a pair of heavy oak doors stands slightly open. You press against one, and it groans as it swings open, revealing a long, dark hallway lit by flickering torches.

At the end of the hallway, a huge stone arch stretches before you—like it's waiting for someone brave—or maybe tasty—to walk through.

You step into a big room where the floor is littered with piles of dusty armor and rusty old swords. It's like a lost-and-found for unlucky knights.

Your heart pounds. You hold your breath and listen carefully... and that's when you hear it—a deep, steady sound echoing through the cavern.

WHOOOSH... WHOOOSH...

Each breath is so powerful you can feel the warm air brush across your cheek from around the corner.

You gulp, your throat suddenly dry. You can't see him yet, but you feel it in your bones—whatever is waiting around that corner has to be the dragon.

You squeeze one eye shut and try to imagine what you're about to face. In your mind, he appears with dark green scales that shimmer like wet leaves, pointy claws that could scratch diamonds, and thick smoke curling from his nostrils as if he's practicing for a fire-breathing contest.

I'm not sure if I'm ready for this, you think nervously, your heart thumping like a drum inside your chest.

 **Turn to page 56.**

 The Library of Lost Relics ◈

You reach a big wooden door labeled **Library**.

"This way," she whispers, as you push it open.

Inside, the library is lit by rows of torches, casting a soft glow across the room. It is so dim in the library that when you look up, it seems like the books go on and on forever into the darkness. On the first floor, rows of glass cases sparkle on every table.

You look into the first case. Inside lies a pair of scuffed leather shoes.

The fairy floats beside you smiling. **"These are Wingswift Shoes,"** she explains. **"Anyone who wears them can run faster than the wind!"**

You look closely and think, *They don't look like much, but they could be helpful if they really work.*

You tiptoe to the next case, where a silver cup shines. **"That's the Death Seeker's Goblet,"** the fairy says, tapping the glass. **"If you pour a drink in here and it turns purple, you know it's poison."**

A few steps later, you see a crystal rock in its own case. The fairy points and explains, **"Don't be fooled by its looks—this is the Honest Heart Stone. Hold it in your hand, and you simply cannot tell a lie."**

Finally, you stop before an empty case. It looks like there's nothing inside until the fairy waves her hand and the air shimmers.

"This is an Invisibility Cloak," she whispers. **"Slip it on, and no one can see you!"**

You take a deep breath, your heart thumping with excitement. Two items seem to be calling to you.

Do you:

- Put on the Wingswift Shoes and hope they help you run fast? (Turn to page 30)
- Slip into the Invisibility Cloak and sneak up on the dragon? (Turn to page 38)

⚡ The Zap ⚡

"Thank you, kind elf, but I can't be distracted from finding the castle. It is my only way home." you say as kindly as you can.

His cheerful eyes dim like someone just turned off his sparkle switch.

"I was really hoping you'd answer my riddle," he whispers in a low growl.

Quietly, he pulls a pointy wooden wand out of his pocket. It's not very big—more like a large popsicle stick —but somehow it feels like you should worry.

"Wait!" you cry out, your voice turns squeaky like a rubber duck. **"What are you going to do with that wand?"**

But the elf only shakes his head and stays silent.

Your stomach does a backflip. *Okay—time to go.* You spin around and dash toward the little door, your backpack bouncing and arms waving to keep balance.

Just as you reach the exit—**ZAP!**

A strange jolt tickles the backs of your legs.

Everything goes black.

When you wake up, you're lying on a soft patch of moss in the woods. You realize that you're not far from the library and your house.

Your heart races as you scramble to your feet and check your backpack.

Please still be there. Please still be there.

You unzip your backpack. Your eyes widen.

The ancient book, **Whispering Woods: Tales of Myths and Magic**, and even the silver feather—both gone.

You blink in the sunlight. Everything is quiet.

Was that all a dream? Or did an elf just zap me out of a magical tree tunnel?

Either way, you're home—for now.

THE END

\!/ The Fairy Kisses \!/

"**Wait, traveler!**" cries the fairy, wings fluttering, leaving a trail of blue fairy dust behind her. "**What's that in your back pocket? Show me!** she growls. **Make the wrong choice and it will toad-ally not be your day.**" The fairy growls again and points her tiny wand at you.

Your heart thumps in your chest. You'd rather not be turned into a warty toad, so you carefully pull the silver feather from your pocket and hold it out.

The fairy's eyes grow big, and her tiny mouth splits into a huge grin. She zooms forward and plants a dozen little fairy kisses on your nose. "**I'm so glad you've arrived!**" she chirps, bouncing with excitement. "**Ever since I was a little fairy, I've heard stories that one day a brave traveler would come carrying an eagle feather, just like this one, and save our land!**"

Her wings droop, and she tugs at a brown leaf tangled in her hair. "**Years ago, I was captured and brought to an evil wizard,**" she says sadly. With tears in her eyes, she sobs, "**The wizard cursed me to guard the dragon. His curse holds me prisoner in this castle until one day the dragon leaves or dies.**"

She looks up at you, her voice cracking, "**I've longed to be free. Please... can you help me?**"

Do you:

 **Decide to find the dragon?** (Turn to page 42)

Decide to use your wish to set the fairy free? (Turn to page 90)

❦ The Red Feather ❦

"**A book!**" you shout.

The Woodland Elf claps his hands, bouncing with joy. "**You're correct!**" he cheers, spinning so hard his leather hat falls sideways. "**For your courage and smarts, I can grant you one wish by enchanting any object you choose. Is there something you'd like me to enchant?**"

You pause, then unzip your backpack and pull out the silver feather the eagle gave you. "**This,**" you say, holding it out carefully.

The elf leans in, eyes wide in surprise. "**Where did you find this feather?**" he asks, nearly tripping over his own excitement.

You grin and tell him about the sky-high trip with the eagle. The elf bows so deeply his nose nearly taps the ground. "**You truly are the one our legend foretold,**" he whispers with awe, and maybe a little extra drama.

He pulls a twisty wooden wand from his pocket. You hold the silver feather steady as he touches it with the wand's tip and murmurs a spell that sounds like a sneeze in another language.

ZING!

A flash of light shoots out like a magical camera flash. When the glow fades, the feather, once silver, is now a deep red.

"**This feather now holds the power to grant one wish. It could help you defeat the dragon,**" the elf explains proudly. "**When you're ready, grasp it tightly and whisper your wish.**"

"This must be what the eagle meant when he said, 'One wish awaits the brave!" you blurt out.

"Thank you!" you cheer, tucking the enchanted feather into your back pocket. You reach for the small door, ready to go full hero mode.

But just as you step through, the elf calls out, **"Wait!"**

You turn back.

"Long ago, a knight broke off one of the dragon's scales, so the dragon wears a jeweled collar around his neck to cover his weak spot. Good luck, traveler!" With a wave and a strange smile, the elf sends you on your way.

You leave the elf's cozy tree home and follow the winding path toward the castle—your adventure finally beginning.

Watch out, dragon. You've got a feather and you're not afraid to use it, you laugh to yourself.

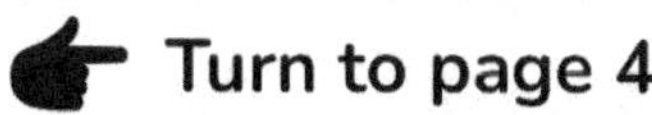 **Turn to page 44.**

You follow the sound of the dragon's breath until you get to a large room. The moment you've been waiting for has finally arrived—You... in the dragon's lair.

You take a bold step forward... and immediately trip over a rusty helmet.

CLANG! CLATTER! BONK!

The helmet rolls away like it's trying to escape what happens next.

Oops. So much for a quiet, heroic entrance.

Before you can scramble to your feet, a loud sound shatters the silence.

"RROOOAAARRRR!"

The dragon wakes up, his giant head rising up from the shadows. Scales glitter like green gemstones— and his eyes, bright as gold, lock onto you. **"Who dares enter my chamber?"** the mighty dragon booms.

You swallow hard, then find your voice. **"It is I... the one who has come to defeat you!"**

The dragon flops back down onto his treasure pile. His eyes narrow as he sizes you up. Then—he laughs deeply and replies, **"Defeat me? You're just big enough for a snack! How do you plan to do that?"**

Just then, the dragon's ears twitch at a soft shuffle behind him. As he stands and turns his head, you see it! The ruby collar slides up his scaly neck, revealing a tiny gap in his armor-like scales.

His weak spot!

Your pulse quickens. This is your chance.

Do you:

👉 **Run up the stairs? (Turn to page 58)**
👈 **Go under the dragon? (Turn to page 60)**

(Turn to page 58)
(Turn to page 60)

You spot a shiny sword by the stairs and snatch it up. Before the dragon can react, you dash up the twisty staircase that ends right above his thick neck.

At the top, you spot him below, standing on a heap of gold like he's the king of the world.

You stand up tall and boldly think, *Time to be brave.*

You leap from the stairs and land right on the dragon's scaly green head.

He thrashes, trying to shake you off, but you hang on, gripping his collar.

Then you spot it again…

A tiny gap in his scales, right where the ruby collar once covered it. You raise the sword, ready to strike…

"STOP!" the dragon roars. Steam puffs from his nose. **"Spare me, and I'll grant you any wish you desire!"**

You freeze. The Woodland Elf told you to defeat him, but this dragon doesn't look evil now—just tired and maybe a little dramatic. Plus, killing a creature isn't really your thing.

Slowly, you slide down his leg and land among the treasure. You place the sword on the floor and look up.

The dragon lowers his head until his golden eyes meet yours. **"You kept your word,"** he says softly. **"Now I'll keep mine. What do you wish for?"**

Do you:

👉 Ask the dragon to fly far away and never to
return? (Turn to page 66)
👉 Ask the dragon to send you home?
(Turn to page 62)
👉 Let the dragon tell his side of the story.
(Turn to page 70)

 The Snack Attack

You dash across the treasure pile, diving for a shiny dagger near the dragon's wing—but uh-oh... he sees you!

"Too slow, snack-size!" he growls, scooping you up by your backpack like a kitten in trouble.

Your heart nearly explodes.

*Think, THINK, **THINK**!*

"Wait!" you squeak. **"Don't eat me—I've got something even tastier!"**

The dragon pauses, lowering his scaly green head until his golden eyes are level with yours. He snorts, and a swirl of hot steam surrounds you, making you wipe sweat from your forehead.

"If you try to trick me," he booms, **"I'll lock you up in the dungeon forever."**

"I promise I'm not tricking you!" you gasp. **"If you put me down, I can give you a peanut butter and jelly sandwich."**

He sets you down gently with a curious look in his eyes. You unzip your backpack, like it's a treasure chest, and hold up the gooey prize. Your saved sandwich—bread perfectly crustless, peanut butter spread thick, jelly just right.

The dragon leans forward, sniffs once... and before you can blink, his forked tongue darts out and slurps the sandwich right from your hand.

He lets out a happy chuckle that echoes through the chamber.

"I have never tasted anything so yummy!" he bellows.

"More! More!"

Do you:

👉 **Wish you could go home fast! (Turn to page 64)**
👉 **Ask the dragon not to eat you. (Turn to page 68)**

The Surprise

You pause, tired from your adventure, dreaming of your warm bed and maybe a snack. *Saving magical creatures is hard work*, you think.

You look up at the dragon.

"Please, mighty dragon," you whisper, **"I want to go home, but I'm worried you may still harm the magical creatures."**

The dragon snorts gently, more like a sleepy cow than a fire-breathing beast, and lowers his head. **"You came all this way to stop me... and now you want to leave?"** he rumbles. **"It isn't *me* hurting the creatures."**

"Wait—what?" You open your mouth to ask more, but the dragon lifts a wing as if to say, **"Shhh."**

Then he blinks three times, slowly—like he's casting the world's fanciest eyelash spell.

Everything around you fades into soft darkness.

Then...

You're back in the library, in your cozy spot, with the familiar smell of old books.

You rub your eyes and look down.

The red feather is still in your hand—glowing just enough to say:

"This isn't over."

And you know it isn't.

THE END

 The Dragon's Chef 

Before the dragon can ask for more sandwiches, you quickly hold up the glowing red feather, ready to whisper your wish to go home.

"I wish to go—"

SWOOSH!

The dragon's tongue snatches the feather right out of your hand like a sticky lizard ninja.

"Hey!" you yell, stumbling back.

The dragon's eyes darken—no longer looking kind. **"You tricked me!"** he growls. **"You never planned to stay. You were going to leave me hungry!"**

He lifts the feather with a sly grin and says, **"I hold the wishing feather now and I want to make you my new peanut butter and jelly sandwich chef forever!"**

Before you can even blink, a strange tug pulls at your belly—it's like being yanked by an invisible rope. The room around you swirls and fades.

Then—**POP!** You land on your feet inside a warm, cozy kitchen tucked deep within the castle walls.

You look down. You're wearing a white apron with the words **"Dragon Chef"** stitched in sparkly thread. In front of you are endless rows of sliced bread stacked as high as your elbows. On shelves behind you sit towers of peanut butter jars and glittering rows of jelly in every color—grape, strawberry, even glittery golden plum!

You spin around, searching wildly. **"My backpack!"** you cry—but it's gone. You pat your pockets—no feather.

"Oh no," you whisper.

You're stuck.

Then you hear it. The dragon, humming, his footsteps getting louder...

Do you:

👉 Sneak out of the kitchen? (Turn to page 78)
👉 Keep making sandwiches and wait for a chance to escape? (Turn to page 80)

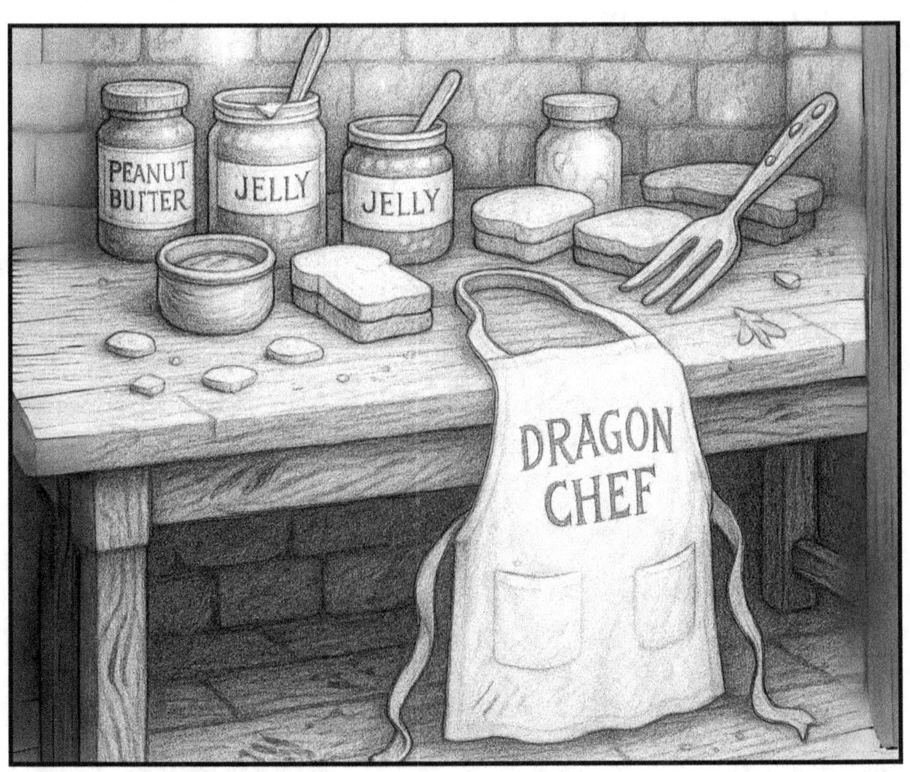

⊹ The Compass ⊹

You look up at the dragon, crouching in the moonlight. You unzip your backpack and pull out the old book with the map.

Opening the map carefully, you point to a sketch of a dragon sitting on a mountain.

The dragon's eyes sparkle. **"That's my home!"** he gasps. **"A wizard cast an invisibility spell around it, and I could never find it again!"**

Just then, you remember the compass tucked inside your backpack. You rummage through it, pushing aside your crustless peanut butter and jelly sandwich. You pull out the compass—and the glowing red feather that's resting beside it.

Holding out the compass, you say, **"I can use my one wish from the elf to help this compass guide you home."**

The dragon's eyes widen, **"What do you mean, your one wish from the elf? Don't you know the feather already holds the power to grant a wish to whoever holds it?"** The dragon looks at you and squints his eyes in doubt, **"At least... I hope the feather was given and not taken!"**

You freeze, realizing that sneaky elf had been up to no good—the only thing he did was turn the feather red and cheat you out of your prize for answering the riddle!

"The silver eagle gave it to me as a gift," you say, a little embarrassed.

The dragon bows his head in thanks. **"Then, I am honored that you would use your wish on me,"** he says softly.

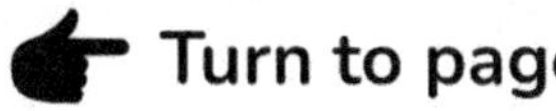

You carefully say to the red feather, **"Make this compass point to the dragon's home."**

The feather glows brightly, and you both have to look away. The compass rattles in your hand, its needle spinning wildly like a race car, until it suddenly stops—now pointing northeast.

You place the compass gently into the dragon's big, clawed hand.

"I know the way home now!" the dragon cheers, joy rumbling in his voice.

👉 **Turn to page 74.**

"I would be glad to help you, as long as you don't eat me," you say bravely, clutching the red feather in one hand.

The dragon snorts a gentle puff of warm air and shakes his head. **"Eat you? I was just kidding,"** he rumbles softly. **"I'm not here to hurt anyone. In fact, I'm a vegetarian—meat makes me very, very sneezy!"**

You stare, wide-eyed and reply, **"A... a vegetarian dragon?"**

The dragon nods, a small plume of smoke drifting from his nostrils. **"Yes! But lately my magic food fountain has been broken, and I can't summon anything to eat."**

You glance at the red feather in your hand, still tingling from the elf's spell. You grin at the dragon. **"I think I can help with that—as long as you can help me get home,"** you say, voice gentle but firm.

"Of course, I have just the thing," he says, pointing his wing at a large golden mirror sparkling in the light. **"Walk through and it will send you anywhere you ask."**

You nod in agreement. Holding the feather firmly, you lean toward the fountain and say, **"Fix the magic food fountain."**

A soft glow spreads from the feather's tip into the fountain's bubbling water. The fountain shimmers and sparkles.

The dragon smiles and says, **"Now, fountain— make me some of those yummy peanut butter and jelly sandwiches!"**

Right before your eyes, slices of bread appear, peanut butter oozes out just right, and ribbons of sweet jelly swirl together. Perfect sandwiches stack themselves on the water's surface, floating like little boats.

The dragon claps his big claws together in joy. **"You've saved my tummy and the fountain!"** he booms with a laugh.

With a quick flick of his long tongue, he snatches a sandwich and gently places it in your hand. **"Please, enjoy a peanut butter and jelly sandwich with me,"** he says with a wide, toothy grin.

You look down at the sandwich... and spot a shiny drop of dragon drool glistening on the crust. *Yuck.* You wrinkle your nose a little, but think, *you should take a bite to be polite.* You lift it to your mouth and take a small nibble.

The dragon watches you and nods happily as he chomps into one of his own sandwiches.

 **Turn to page 76.**

 The Villain or Not? 

You pause and look at the dragon and bravely ask, **"Mighty dragon, can I ask you a question first?"**

The great dragon tilts his head, his golden eyes big and sad. He lowers his head until his eyes are level with your not-so-giant face.

Your knees wobble a little, but you stand firm like a snack-sized hero. To your surprise, he nods **yes**.

"The Woodland Elf said I was the chosen one," you say, scratching your head. **"He told me you were hurting magical creatures. I thought I had to stop you... but now I'm not so sure that's the whole story. Can you tell me your side?"**

The dragon chuckles—a full belly laugh—and for a second, you're sure he might blast fire out his nose. **"That Elf?"** he snorts. **"He works for the true villian —an evil wizard who will do anything to rule our world. Tricking travelers like you is part of the fun for Marrick the Elf."**

Your eyes widen. *What a plot twist!* **"I knew something wasn't right! Can I help you defeat Marrick and the wizard?"** you ask with excitement.

"Only the Orb of Destiny can find the wizard... but it's been lost for years," he says sadly.

You nearly bounce out of your boots. **"I KNOW where it is!"** you shout. **"It was outside the tunnel that brought me here! I can summon it with my feather!"**

Without waiting for the dragon's reply, or even thinking about how you will get home, you pull out your glowing red feather and shout, **"Bring me the Orb of Destiny!"**

FLASH!

In an instant, the orb appears—glimmering with golden light and looking completely destiny-approved.

 **Turn to the next page.**

The Ride Home 

The dragon's eyes glimmer. **"You used your enchanted feather to bring me the orb,"** he says, amazed. **"I owe you a favor. Now, what's your wish?"**

You pause. Sure, getting home quickly sounds great, but so does flying through the sky on a dragon with giant glimmering wings.

You clear your throat and ask, **"Um...mighty dragon— can you fly me home?"**

The dragon lowers his head so you're nose-to-nose. After a short pause, he says with a toothy smile, **"Climb aboard, hold tight and no snacks during takeoff."**

Grinning, you grab his jeweled collar and hop onto his shoulder like a dancer with perfect balance.

With a swipe of his claw, the dragon presses a hidden switch tucked behind the curtain—*because, of course, dragons always have secret exits*—and a section of the stone wall slides open.

WHOOSH! With a thunderous flap, you soar into the starry sky.

The wind tickles your face. Stars sparkle like they're flickering candles. Below, the Whispering Woods look like a dark maze.

"This is AWESOME!" you shout in the wind, trying not to fall off from excitement.

Soon, your town comes into view—the library, your street and your house!

The dragon gently lands at the edge of the woods.

You slide off, heart racing. **"Thanks for the ride,"** you say, hugging his giant snout.

He plucks a little ruby stone from his collar. **"If you ever need me, hold the ruby and call out my name— Emberwing. Then, meet me at midnight at the entrance of your woods. I'll come as soon as I can."**

With one last flap, he's gone—leaving you grinning under the stars.

 The Goblet

You smile up at the dragon. **"Now that you can go home, please stay there and stop scaring all the magical creatures, okay?"**

The dragon lowers his giant, scaly head and rumbles, **"I only fought back when others attacked me! The real troublemaker is the wizard and his followers. I'll deal with them soon."**

A nasty wizard and a lying elf? What's next—a grumpy troll with dance moves?

The dragon's eyes twinkle. **"But first, what would you like as a reward? Silver? Jewels? A golden toilet seat?"**

You laugh and shake your head. **"I'm glad you'll handle the wizard. Right now, I think I just want to go home."**

The dragon nods, as if he completely understands. Then he points at a fancy cup beside you. It shimmers in the light, slowly filling with a cool, silvery liquid. **"Drink from this goblet,"** he rumbles, **"and speak the place you wish to go. It will take you there."**

You lift the magical cup, taking a small sip—hoping it's not, you know, poison or dragon mouthwash and whisper, **"Home."**

Your toes tingle, the ground whooshes upward like a magical elevator— **POOF!**

You blink... and suddenly, you're back in your room. Morning sunshine, cozy blankets, and your mom calling, **"Time to get up, sleepyhead!"**

You sit up, rubbing your eyes, wondering, *was it all just a dream?*

Then you spot on your pillow a single gold coin, engraved with a teeny-tiny dragon scale.

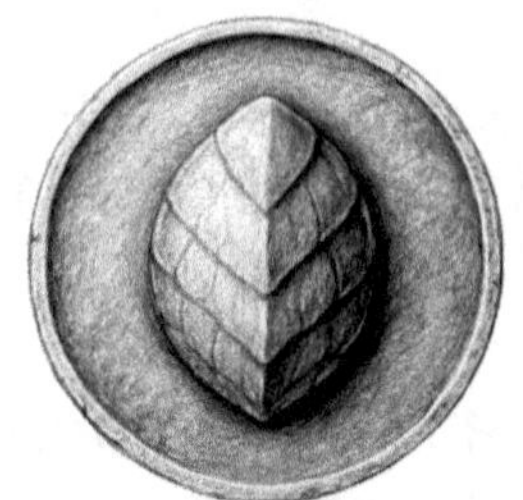

Not a dream after all.

And one big question still buzzes in your brain—
Now what about that wizard...?

You take a deep breath and ask, **"Majestic dragon—if you're a vegetarian, who's been hurting the magical creatures?"**

The dragon freezes mid-chew. **"No one's ever asked me that,"** he says, surprised. **"It's not me—it's an evil wizard trying to take over the land."**

Your eyes go wide—so *THAT'S what's really going on!* you think.

"I'm sorry I tried to fight you," you say. **"I didn't know the truth. I hope you can find the wizard and stop him."**

The dragon smiles gently and nods. **"I accept your apology. I'm one of the magical creatures too. My goal has always been to stop the wizard."**

You're glad the dragon has a plan and you decide to leave the wizard hunting to him.

"I'm tired," you admit. **"I think it's time I go home."**

The dragon nods, then points to the gold mirror he showed you before.

"When you're ready to go home," he says kindly, **"Just step through this magic mirror and picture in your mind where you want it to take you."**

You take a deep breath, hug the dragon's scaly leg. Then you walk towards the mirror and carefully step through the soft glass.

Home! you shout in your mind, picturing your backyard.

In a flash of light,
you blink and find
yourself standing in your
very own backyard.

The sun is shining, birds
are chirping, and your
garden gnome watches
over the flower beds.

You look down at your
hand and you see a
PB&J sandwich with one
bite missing.

Best. Adventure. Ever.

THE END

 # The Escape 

You tiptoe to the kitchen door, careful not to knock over a wobbly tower of jelly jars. The dragon's hum echoes down the hallway—low and bouncy, like he's in a great mood.

Good, you think. He won't suspect a thing.

You peek into the hall and it's empty. Now's your chance!

You slip off your apron, toss it onto the counter, then dash out the door. Your footsteps echo on the stone floor as you dart down a twisty hallway. The castle is a maze of glowing torches, whispering shadows, and strange surprises.

First stop? A hallway full of creepy mirrors—each showing a different you (one even has broccoli in its teeth. Ew).

Next? A mountain of giant dragon slippers—all REALLY, REALLY, HUGE.

At last, you skid to a stop. In front of you stands a large wooden door. Etched across the center of the door is the outline of a glowing feather.

This has to be your way out. You reach for the door handle, hoping it's not locked. **Click**, it opens with a **creak**.

Inside is a round room glowing with soft blue light.

And there it is—a mirror laying on the ground, filled with liquid instead of glass, like someone melted an ice cube.

You step closer, your heart thumping like a marching band in your chest.

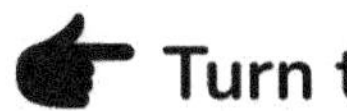 **Turn to page 84.**

 # The New Chance 

You sigh and tighten your Dragon Chef apron. **"Fine."** you grumble. **"One or two sandwiches won't hurt... unless I'm stuck here forever."**

You start spreading peanut butter on one slice, jelly on the other—classic strawberry, seeds and all. Perfect corners. You press them together gently, making sure the corners match just right.

One sandwich done.

You keep going, making each one neater than the last. The kitchen fills with the warm, nutty smell of roasted peanuts and sweet sugar. *It's actually kind of comforting... if you weren't forced to be here.*

Just then, the dragon's giant head pokes through the doorway. His tongue zips out—**SLURP, SLURP, SLURP!**—and three sandwiches disappear.

"Delicious!" he booms. **"You nailed the jelly-to-bread ratio! You're a natural, little chef!"**

You smile weakly. **"Glad you like them."**

But inside? **PANIC MODE.**

There has to be a way out of here—come on, think! Your eyes dart from shelf to shelf: peanut butter, jelly, crates of bread, a cupboard full of dragon-scale plates—nothing...

Then, as you lift a slice of bread, a tiny red glow peeks out from beneath the strawberry jelly jar.

You freeze. No way... could it be?

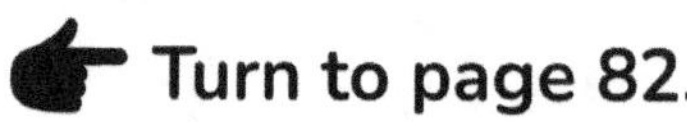 **Turn to page 82.**

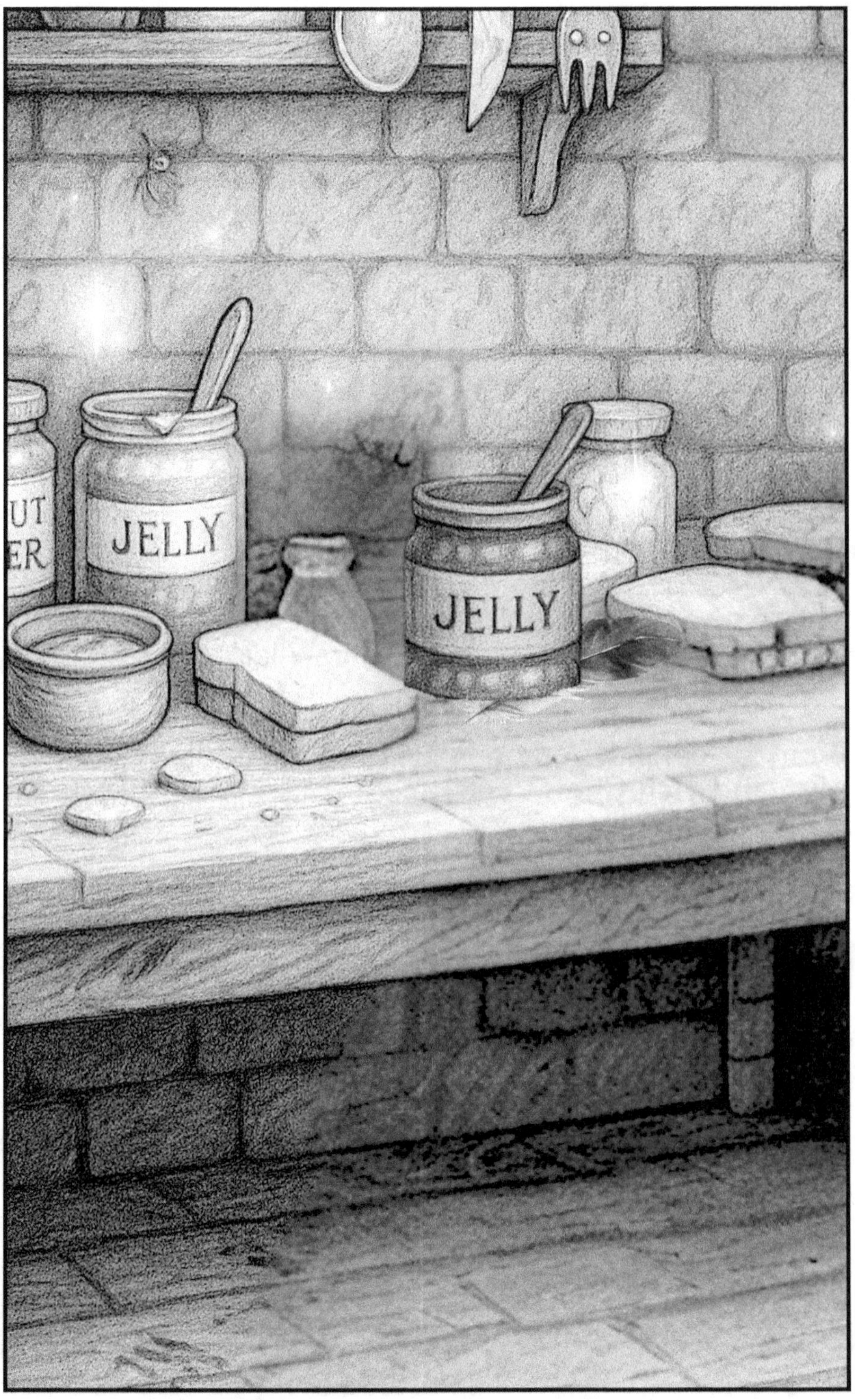
UT
ER
JELLY
JELLY

✦ The Surprise ✦

You slide the jelly jar aside, heart thumping.

There it is—the red feather!

How did the dragon drop it? Never mind—take the win. You snatch it up, clutching it like treasure.

You peek at the dragon—still happily chomping sandwiches like it's lunchtime forever.

You glance back at the feather—but wait… didn't the dragon already use the wish? You hope there's just one more wish left for you, and you whisper, **"I wish to go home."**

WHOOOSH!

The feather lights up like a firecracker! The room spins with sandwiches, shelves, jelly jars—it's a PB&J tornado!

From far behind, you hear the dragon shout, **"Wait! My Sandwich Chef!"**

FLASH!

You land softly on mossy ground. The stars twinkle, the wind whispers, and your backpack's back where it belongs.

You made it home.

The feather glows one last time in your hand, then gently floats into the sky and sparkles away.

You smile and think. *Maybe one day you'll go back. But for now? It feels good to be home… and maybe even time for a snack.*

🏁 THE END 🏁

ANUT
TTER
JELLY
JELLY

The Mirror 

A strange voice echoes around you, **"This is your way home. Go now—before you're stuck forever!"**

You don't even think.

You leap into the mirror.

WHOOSH!

The world spins like a sparkly tornado. Wind in your ears—stars in your eyes.

THUMP!

You land on soft moss.

You blink.

Above you: the moon.

Around you: familiar trees.

Under you: definitely not the castle floor.

You're back in the woods by your home. Your backpack is back on... but no feather, no dragon, no glitter jelly.

Just you. You're home.

You breathe deeply, grinning.

You made it.

 **THE END**

You blink and sit up slowly on the library's second floor. Your head's still spinning like you just got off a merry-go-round.

It's quiet—too quiet. Then...

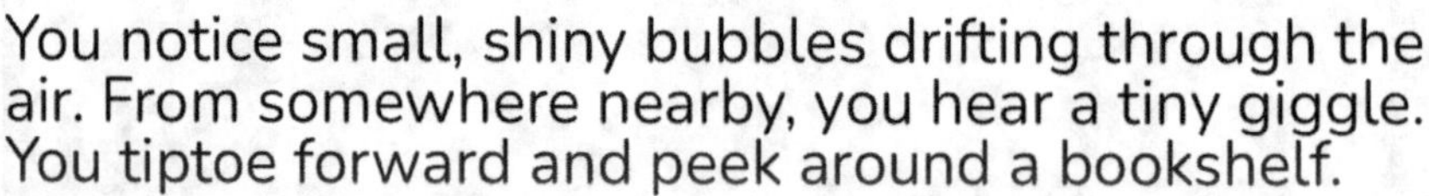

Bubbles.

You notice small, shiny bubbles drifting through the air. From somewhere nearby, you hear a tiny giggle. You tiptoe forward and peek around a bookshelf.

Nobody. Just more floating bubbles.

You decide to check the lever from the secret tunnel and it's stuck. The book is gone. But the bubbles? Still floating, still sparkling, still magical.

One drifts right up to your face. Inside it, you swear you see a teeny-tiny fairy waving at you.

You smile wide at the bubble. **"Thank you,"** you whisper.

The bubble pops on your fingertip, leaving a sparkling blue droplet that quickly fades. You sigh, tuck your hands in your pockets, and head for the stairs.

The tunnel might be gone. The book might have vanished. But you know this adventure isn't really over. You glance back one last time... then grin.

Now to head home and figure out who's going to believe you!

DRAGONSPIRE

 **The Shoes** 

The fairy flutters up to you, eyes shining. **"You did it! You freed the land from the dragon!"**

"Thanks to your help," you say with a grin.

She tilts her head. **"Would you like to stay here with me? There's so much more to explore."**

You shake your head, hugging your arms against your chest. **"Thank you, but I'm ready to go home."**

The fairy nods and points at your feet. **"Your Wingswift Shoes have one more use,"** she explains. **"Start running, think of home, and they'll carry you there!"**

You feel the shoes' magic hum against your feet.

"Ready?" she whispers.

"Ready," you reply.

With a joyful whoosh, you dash forward, the world blurring by. You think about home, especially your adventures in the woods. In an instant, you're back on the wooded path by your home. You can see the old brick library with its ivy-covered walls and flickering lamps on the other end of the path.

A big smile spreads across your face. You made it home and faster than you ever imagined. You look down at the trail and notice a surprise. You wiggle your toes in the worn leather Wingswift **Shoes**, and think, *"I wonder if the shoes still…"*

🧚 The Freedom Of The Fairy 🧚

You feel a lump in your throat. The little fairy deserves to return to her home, but you're not sure how to help her.

The fairy sees your confusion. **"Show me your feather. I have a feeling that it might hold magic that we can use."** You hold out the silver feather.

She touches it with her wand and it starts to glow. **"Just as I thought—a silver eagle feather! Any feather taken from the eagle or the eagle gives away, holds one wish for the person who holds it. Many silver eagles have been hunted for their magical feathers, and Skyrider is the only one left,"** she says sadly with small blue tears streaming down her face.

You feel immense sadness for Skyrider, the grand silver eagle. **"I'll use my wish to send you home,"** you say.

The fairy flutters around and says excitedly, **"I have an idea. If we both hold the feather and whisper 'home,' it might grant both our wishes."**

Just as you raise the feather—

BOOM! A loud **crash!**

You spin around and there he is—the dragon! He must of heard us and he looks furious.

You squeeze your eyes shut and hold the feather together with the fairy. **"I wish to go home!"** you both shout, and then everything spins and then stops.

You sit up in bed, blinking in the morning light. From your doorway, you hear your sister laughing, **"You were yelling 'dragon!' in your sleep!"**

You smile. *Could it really have been a dream?*

Then you spot blue sparkles on your hand.

Fairy dust.

A flicker of green zips past your window, sprinkling glittery blue dust behind. **"My name is Luna and it was nice to meet you!"**

"Wait!" you call, but the fairy is already flying off toward the woods.

You smile and tuck one last speck of fairy dust into your pocket.

If she ever needs help again...

You'll be ready.

 **THE END**

 The Map

"**A map!**" you exclaim, feeling a burst of hope.

The Woodland Elf looks down at his toes and shakes his head slowly. His tiny shoulders slump like someone just told him the playground is closed.

"**You were so close,**" he says softly, "**but not quite right.**"

You stare at him, your brain doing somersaults. *Wait… that wasn't it? But it had to be!* you think in a panic.

The elf pulls a twisty wooden wand from his pocket. His sparkly blue eyes shimmer with sadness.

"**If you can't solve my riddle, then you are not the right one to save the magical creatures,**" he explains. He hesitates, then adds, "**That means you will not face the wizard—I mean dragon—today.**"

You blink. Hard.

"**What do you mean—wizard?**" you ask, your voice cracking like a potato chip.

The elf glares at you with frustration. Then, to your total shock, he lets out a low growl. Yup. An actual growl.

"**I didn't mean to say that!**" he shouts, his voice suddenly deeper, grumpier, and about five levels scarier.

Oh no. He's either possessed... or very hangry.

You feel your heart sink as the elf raises his wand. He begins to chant strange, whispery words.

FLASH!

A bright light surrounds you, and for a moment, you feel weightless—like floating inside a bubble.

Then—**POOF!**

When the light fades, you're standing in the familiar halls of your town library once more. The smell of old books and dust fills your nose. Somewhere in the distance, someone coughs politely.

You blink. You're back.

You unzip your backpack and peek inside. The book is gone!

In its place lies the feather, but it's sparkle is gone.

You hold it in your hand and whisper, **"Maybe one day I'll solve that riddle... and find the true villain."**

You tuck it away, just in case.

🏁 **THE END** 🏁

 The Exhausted Dragon 🌙

With your Wingswift Shoes laced tight, you and the fairy zoom down the castle hallway to the dragon's cave. Firelight flickers on piles of treasure as the dragon slowly lifts his huge head.

"Ah—I see intruders in my castle!" the dragon growls, his eyes narrowing. **"Tiny thieves! I'll roast you!"**

The dragon sucks in a deep breath, his scaly body shaking. But whoosh! You dash out of the way just in time. The fire blasts past you and hits the wall instead.

"Ha!" you laugh, running in big circles around the dragon's feet. **"You can't catch me!"**

The dragon snarls and leaps at you—but every time it swipes, you're already gone. You zoom past shiny jewels and old broken swords like a blur.

Finally, the dragon drops to his knees, breathing hard. **"Okay! I give up!"** it huffs. **"What do you want? I can't beat you!"**

You stop in front of him, your heart pounding in your chest. **"You have to leave this land and promise never to hurt anyone again,"** you say firmly.

The dragon's tail thumps, and it shakes his great head. **"No, this is my castle,"** it growls. **"You can't make me leave!"**

Your heart races. You know it's time. You reach into your pocket and pull out the silver feather the eagle gave you.

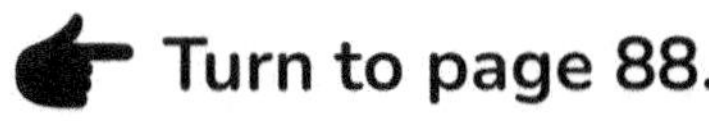

The dragon's eyes go wide with surprise.

You whisper, **"Send the dragon far away—to a place where he can't hurt anyone ever again."**

With a puff of sparkling smoke, the dragon disappears.

The cave falls quiet. You and the fairy cheer and twirl in a happy dance!

👉 **Turn to page 88.**

The Riddle Answer 

You know this is a big task—maybe the most important one of all. You have a real chance to save the creatures of this land… and maybe even get home in one piece.

After a quick breath and one last nervous glance at the elf's wand, you nod.

"Yes," you say bravely, and reach out to shake the little elf's hand.

His fingers are warm and kind of squishy, like a cookie fresh from the oven.

You're ready. *Bring on the riddle.*

The elf straightens his vest, clears his throat, and unrolls an old scroll. In a soft, sing-song voice, he begins to read:

"You see me sitting on a shelf, quiet and still,
Yet filled with adventures waiting to thrill.
Open me up and journeys begin
With dragons, heroes, and worlds hidden within.
What am I?"

He lifts an eyebrow—like he's daring you to sneeze, blink, or guess wrong.

Okay, you realize. *This one's not about snacks. Well, probably not about snacks*, you think as your tummy growls with hunger.

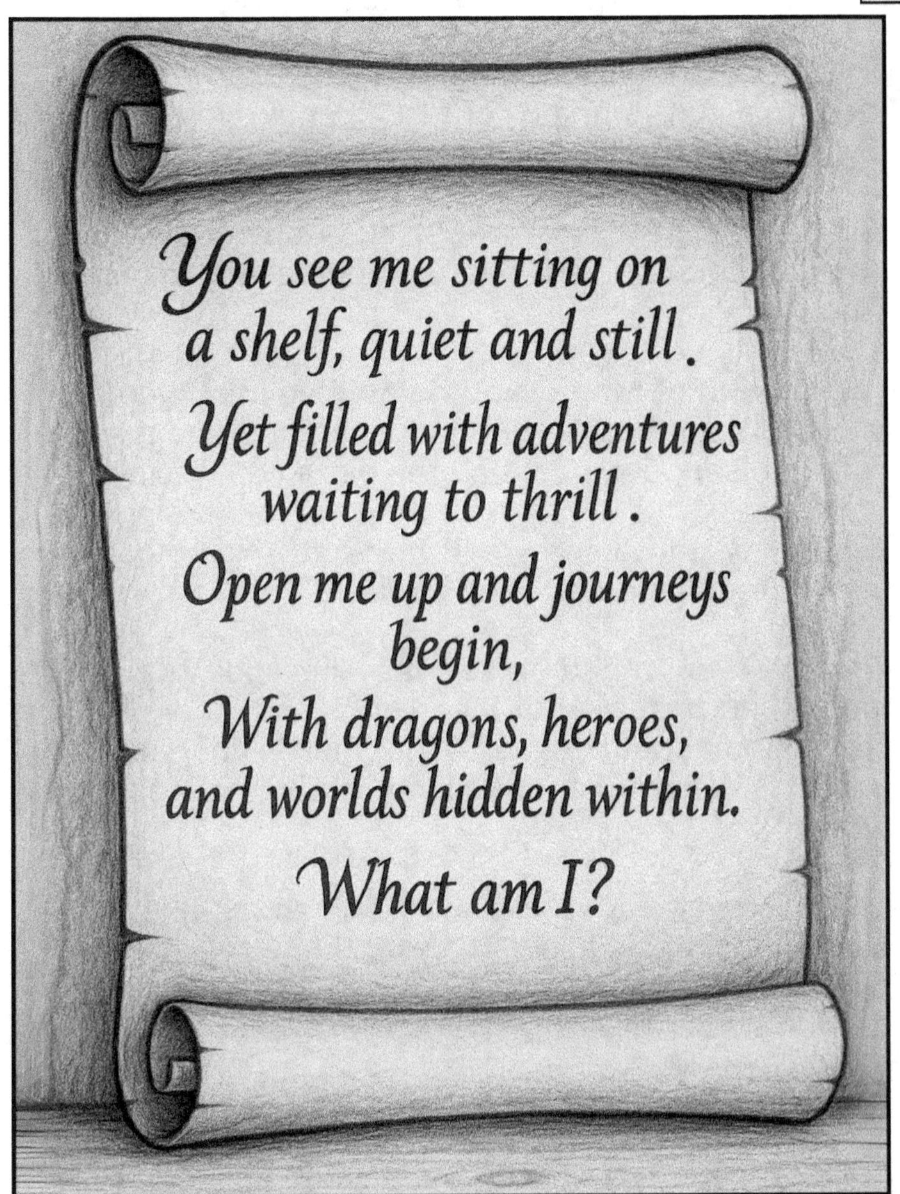

Do you:

👉 Answer the riddle with the word BOOK?
(Turn to page 54)

👉 Answer the riddle with the word MAP?
(Turn to page 92)

The Woodland Elf is beaming like he just won first place in a leaf-jumping contest. **"I knew you'd be brave!"** he exclaims in a squeaky, cheerful voice.

You tilt your head like a confused puppy. *Brave? Is this riddle dangerous?* Then you remember the magical surprise.

"What kind of magic would you give me?" you ask, trying to sound cool—but really hoping it means you can fly, disappear, or eat all the pizza you want.

"Solve my riddle and you'll find out!" He holds out his tiny hand and asks, **"Is it a deal?"**

You open your mouth to say **yes**—because, duh, magical surprises!—but then you pause. There is something about this riddle that makes you feel uneasy. **"What if I answer incorrectly?"** you ask worried.

The elf's smile fades. His shoulders slump like a balloon losing air. In a soft, trembling voice, he whispers, **"Then we will all perish under the dragon's fiery breath."**

Your eyebrows shoot up. *Whoa... that got serious quickly.* **"How do you know it is the dragon up to no good?"** you ask, trying to sound calm.

The elf replies with a strange look on his face. **"An old wizard came by years ago and told me all about the green dragon that lives in DragonSpire Castle,"** he says. **"He also told me that when the dragon gets mad, he flies out of the castle and destroys everything in his sight."**

You blink. *Okay, so this riddle might be important to solve.*

Turn to page 96.

Bonus: The Dragon's Silly Sandwich Recipe

If you ever want to make a snack fit for a dragon, try this fun recipe (no dragon spit required!).

Ingredients:

- 2 slices of bread
- 1 big spoonful of peanut butter or a nut free choice
- 1 swirl of jelly (any flavor-strawberry, grape, or glittery plum)
- 1 silly twist (like rainbow sprinkles, a banana slice smiley face, or mini marshmallows)

Directions:

1. Spread the peanut butter on one slice of bread.
2. Spread the jelly on the other.
3. Add your silly twist.
4. Press them together, cut into shapes, (maybe dragon wings or scales?) and take a bite.

Warning: May cause giggling, magical daydreams, or cravings for adventure.

Glossary

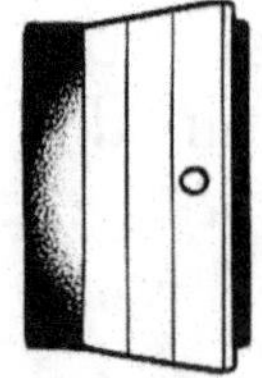

Ajar
A door that's a little bit open, not fully closed.

Chandelier
Fancy light that hangs from the ceiling.

Cloak
A long piece of clothing, like a cape, that keeps you warm or helps you hide.

Courtyard
An open space inside the walls of a castle or big building.

Creature
Any living thing, real or magical, like animals, monsters, or fairies

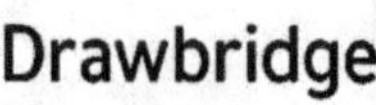

Drawbridge
A bridge at the front of a castle that can be lifted up to block entry.

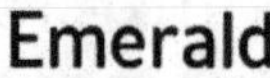

Emerald
A shiny green gemstone.

Enchanted
Something magical, full of spells or wonder.

Gleaming
Shiny and bright, like something polished.

Glossary

Leather
Material made from animal hide, often used for shoes, belts, or armor.
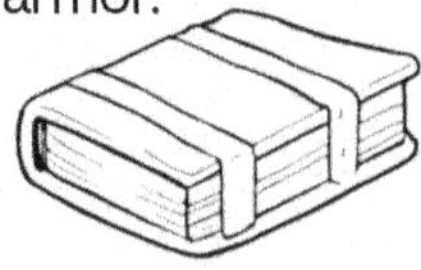
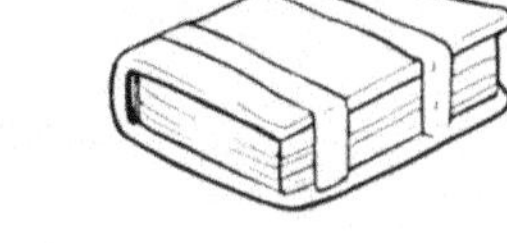

Merchant
A person who sells things, like in a market.

Royalty
Kings, queens, princes, and princesses who rule a kingdom.

Shield
A flat piece of armor carried on the arm to block attacks.

Moat
A wide ditch filled with water around a castle to keep it safe.

Orb
A round ball, often magical or glowing.

Quiver
A bag that holds arrows, usually worn on the back.

Scrolls
Rolled-up pieces of paper or parchment with writing on them.
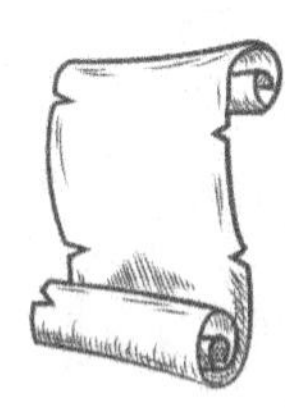

Torches
Sticks with fire on top, used for light.

"Your ideas matter. Your dreams matter.
Keep imagining big—and the world will
make room for them."

Willowsong
Press

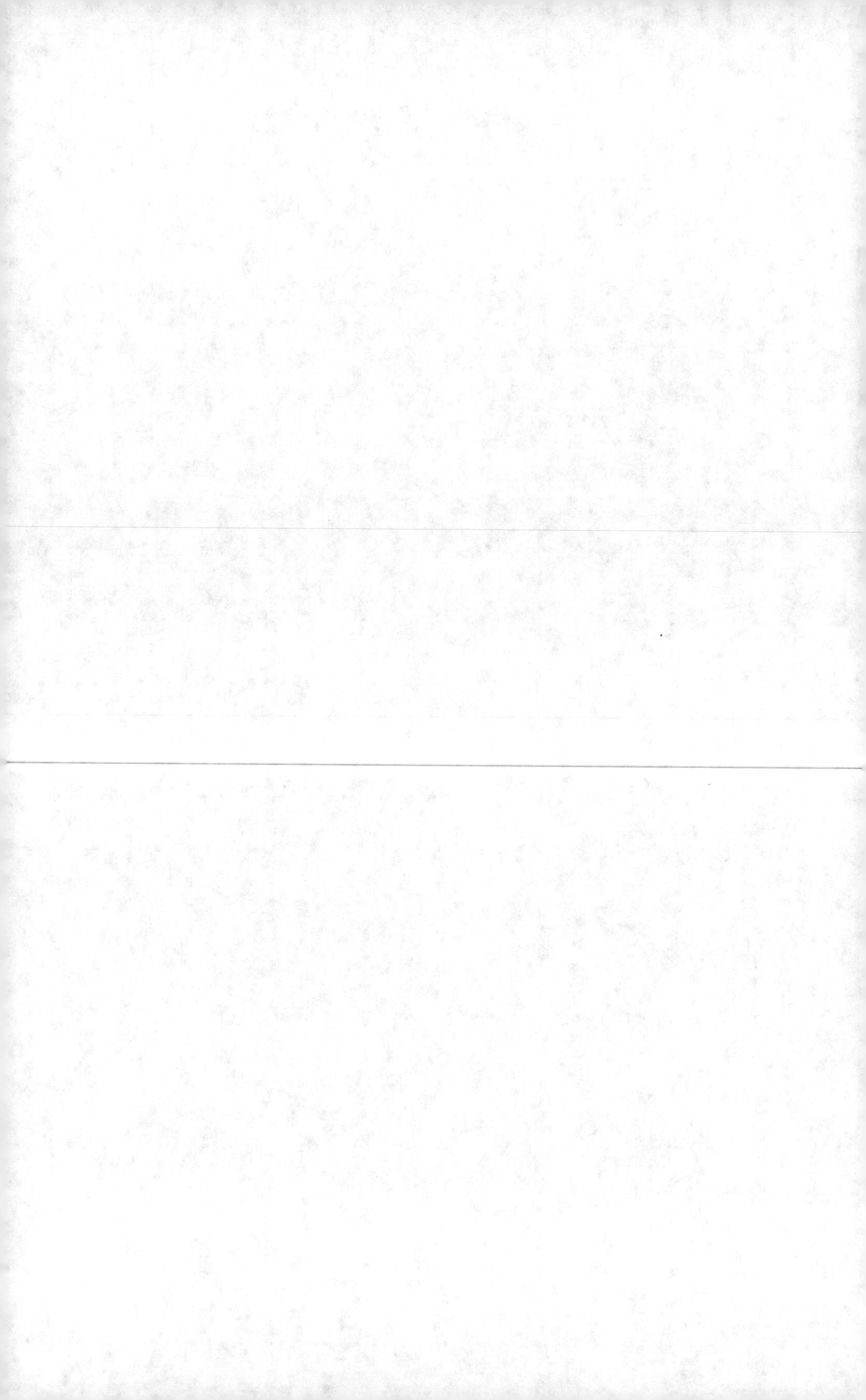